THE
SLIME
FROM THE
BLACK LAGOON®

THE
SLIME
FROM THE
BLACK LAGOON®

by Mike Thaler
Illustrated by Jared Lee

SCHOLASTIC INC.

To Samantha
—M.T.

To Doug and Regina Morgan
—J.L.

SLIME→

Text copyright © 2019 by Mike Thaler
Illustrations copyright © 2019 by Jared Lee

ISBN 978-1-338-56808-0

10 9 8 7 6 5 4 3 2   19 20 21 22 23

Printed in the U.S.A.   40
First printing 2019

CLOUD→   SLIME→

HAPPY
CAT →

CONTENTS

GIDDY
PLANE →

CHAPTER 1
DOWN THE TUBE

Out of all my teachers, the weirdest by far is the science teacher—Mr. Hyde. He wears super-thick glasses that make his eyes look like two fish in a fishbowl. He has long hair that

he combs straight back . . . from his eyebrows! But he acts even stranger than he looks.

He has a skeleton hanging in his room . . . a real one!

IS THIS YOURS?

They say he collects worms, germs, and squirms, bugs and slugs, and keeps them all in his pockets.

8

They say he has jars filled with brains and eyeballs. You feel like you're being watched all the time.

CHAPTER 2
A STICKY SITUATION

Science class is right before lunch. Ecchh!!

Mr. Hyde likes to do really weird experiments. I heard you have to take a microscope into the cafeteria and look for bacteria. Last year, a kid examined a drop of water through the microscope and got so weirded out he didn't drink it for a year.

Once, the class had to hold hands between two electrodes and Mr. Hyde measured how they conducted themselves.

This year, we are all nervously looking forward to an interesting semester.

ZIP!

POP!

BUZZ!

AP!

ELECTRODE

ELECTRODE

13

CHAPTER 3
GOO SIT DOWN

We all get to choose our own seats. I look for one without green goo on it, away from the skeleton. I sit down. The bell rings, and the door slowly opens. Mr. Hyde shuffles in. He looks around the room and rubs his hands together.

"Welcome to science," he chuckles. "Your first project is to create your own slime." Then he rubs his hands together again, rolls his eyes, and chuckles.

CHAPTER 4
A DITHER ABOUT SLITHER

SLIME →

On the bus ride home, all the kids are excited.

I'M THRILLED.

I'M DELIGHTED.

I'M ECSTATIC.

"I'm going to make pink slime with glitter," says Doris.

DORIS →

"Big deal," says Randy. "I'm going to make slime that changes color!"

"Well, I'm going to make glo-slime," says Derek.

BIRD
BUG
TREAT

"Well, I'm going to make go slime," Eric says, smiling.

"What's that?" I ask.

"You make it . . . and it goes."

"Where does it go?" asks Doris.

"It goes after YOU!" shouts Eric, wiggling his fingers.

"Well, I'll make blobby slime that eats your go slime," says Freddy.

 ← MINI SLIME

"What about you, Hubie?" asks Eric.

"I'm going to make slime that minds its own business," I say, and look out the window.

CHAPTER 5
THE MAD SCIENTIST

When I arrive home I get everything I need to make slime.

I borrow Mom's rubber kitchen gloves. I put on Mom's apron, my ski goggles, and my football helmet.

Tailspin sees me and runs under the bed.

I go to my laboratory (the bathroom) and think over all the possibilities. There are hundreds of choices. It's worse than choosing an ice-cream flavor!

Luckily, Mom calls me to dinner.

MAD
SCIENTIST
↓

LABORATORY
RESTRICTED
AREA,
STAY
OUT!

26

←ASSISTANT

27

CHAPTER 6
STUCK IN SLIME

The truth is, I have no idea what kind of slime to make.

As research, I talk Mom into letting me stay up and see *The Slime That Ate Chicago*.

CRUNCH
CRUNCH
CRUNCH

TERRIFYING!

"You are going to have a nightmare, Hubie."

"No, I won't, Mom."

"Yes, you will, Hubie."

"No, I won't."

The movie is about a mad scientist who looks a lot like our science teacher, Mr. Hyde. He wants to invent Super Slime, but instead he invents Supper Slime, and then the slime eats him. He gets really absorbed in his work.

But the slime is still hungry . . . so it goes on to eat Chicago. Luckily, the suburbs give it a stomachache and it dies.

"Okay, Hubie, turn off the television and go to bed."

I brush my teeth, put on my superhero pajamas, turn out the light, and go to sleep.

LIGHT OFF

32

CHAPTER 7
A SLIMEMARE

I fall right asleep and I do have a nightmare. Why are moms always right?

DEEP SLEEP MODE

SHALLOW SLEEP MODE

DOESN'T SLEEP MODE

I am soon in my laboratory, making slime. I just start with a little glo-slime. But instead of putting in glow powder, I pour in grow powder. Then I close the door and go to bed.

FIRE EXTINGUISHER

STANDING ON STOOL

GROW POWDER

SLIME HEAD ⟶

In the morning, when I go back to my laboratory, the room is full of a burbling green slime. It absorbed the whole box of grow powder and wants more. I try to close the door. I push and push . . . but the slime wants out. It eats the door off its hinges and starts looking for other things to devour.

LABORATORY RESTRICTED AREA, STAY OUT!

WHAT HAVE I DONE?

YOU'RE MAD, I TELL YOU, YOU'RE MAD.

35

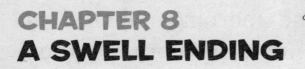

CHAPTER 8
A SWELL ENDING

I dial 911 and soon a SWAT team pulls up. The slime seems to like everything they shoot at it.

Plunk, plunk, plunk. "Yumm!"

There's no stopping it. Call the Slime Squad. Call the Federal Slime Investigators. Call Slimebusters!

Everybody comes to watch. The slime is very social.

It eats up the attention and gets bigger and bigger. It is about to eat me, when I wake up.

How do moms get so smart?

CHAPTER 9
THE OOZE BLUES

I still don't know what kind of slime to make. There is so much to choose from. I could make slim slime or fat slime.

Sticky slime or icky slime, blobby slime or globby slime.

Slime that glows.

Slime that flows.

Slime that changes color.

41

Slime that changes shape.

Slime that changes temperature.

There is a world of slime possibilities. Time is running out for Show and Tell. The clock is ticking.

CHAPTER 10
SLIME TIME

In the morning, on the bus to school, everyone is very secretive. They all sit quietly with mysterious bags, sacks, and boxes on their laps. No one says much, but there sure is a lot of burbling and gurgling going on.

NO TALKING WHATSOEVER ➡

CHAPTER 11
GLOW AND SMELL

It is Show and Tell time.

"Who wants to go first?" asks Mr. Hyde.

Eric's hand shoots up. In his other hand is a green plastic bag.

"Eric," says Mr. Hyde. "Go for it!"

Eric jumps up and walks to the front of the class.

"My slime," he proudly states, "obeys my commands."

BUG ON WRONG PAGE →

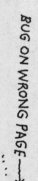

OVER-ANXIOUS →

GREEN PLASTIC → BAG

ANNOYED ↓

46

The class gasps "ohhs" and "ahhs" as Eric slowly opens his green bag and plops a blob of green slime onto the floor.

Blop!

Then he looks down at it and points his finger.

"Sit!" he commands.

The slime slowly settles into a pile.

Triumphantly, Eric walks to the other side of the room.

"Stay!" he shouts.

The slime stays. It doesn't move.

"What else does it do?" asks
Mr. Hyde.

Eric looks at the pile of slime
sitting on the science room floor.

"Not much else," sighs Eric. "But I'm planning to train it to do a dance."

51

"Who's next?" sighs Mr. Hyde. Penny raises her hand.

Eric picks up his slime and slips it back into his green plastic bag.

"Stay," he says as he closes the top.

I WILL.

Derek's slime didn't eat a thing.
He said it wasn't hungry.

Then I have it!
Inspiration has struck!
Eureka!
I'm ready. I can slime with the best of them.
Success is in the bag!

CHAPTER 13
SLIME READY

"Well, Hubie," says Mr. Hyde, rolling his eyes. "It's your turn. What's in your plastic bag?"

I confidently walk to the front of the class. I open my plastic bag and empty nothing onto the table. Everyone looks puzzled.

"I have created *invisible* slime."
I smile.

"I don't see it," says Mr. Hyde.

"Exactly," I say. "It's invisible."

CLAP
CLAP
CLAP
CLAP
CLAP
CLAP

Mr. Hyde chuckles.
The class applauds.
I get a B+ for imagination.
"Science is seventy-five percent
imagination!" says Mr. Hyde.

POTENTIAL
FEAST

61

CHAPTER 14
SLIME ON MY HANDS

Making slime is fun when you do it safely. Here are a few tips for you:

1. Wear gloves and goggles. Wear old clothes or an apron, as well.

2. Use nontoxic and washable glue.

3. Follow the directions carefully—don't skip steps, don't substitute ingredients, and make sure you use the proper measurements. For example, a teaspoon (tsp) is different than a tablespoon (tbs).

4. Chemicals can be harmful. Many slime experts suggest not using borax, as it can cause burns.

5. Have a parent help you. If you experience any symptoms like itching, redness, tingling, or irritation, tell them immediately.

SLIME ⟶

64